I Love You, Baby Deer

I Love You, Baby Deer

By Linda Gilleland

I Love You, Baby Deer

Brown Books Publishing Group
16250 Knoll Trail Drive, Suite 205
Dallas, Texas 75248
www.BrownBooks.com
(972) 381-0009

A New Era in Publishing™

ISBN 978-1-61254-025-2
Library of Congress Control Number: 2011941064

Printing in the United States
10 9 8 7 6 5 4 3 2 1

www.ILoveYouBabyDeer.com

To my husband, Bruce, who has always been
my number one best friend, and to my granddaughter,
Grace, who will forever be the shadow of my heart.

Contents

Prologue

Grace looked down at the table and picked up the worn, faded picture. The colors were not as bright as in the beginning when the picture was new. Grace was eight years old, going on nine, and she never grew tired of looking at the beautiful baby deer and the young puppy that had been her closest friends not so very long ago.

Grace took the picture and walked into the kitchen where Grannie was making her favorite cookies, with lots of icing and sprinkles. Grace loved the farm and all the animals, and it was always a special treat when she got to come and visit her Grannie and Grandpa. She tugged on Grannie's sleeve and held out the picture.

"Tell me the Pineapple story again, Grannie. Tell me about when I was a little girl and Pineapple came to live with me."

"Gracie!" Grannie said. "You should know that story by heart. I have told it to you so many times. You could tell that story to me."

"I know," said Grace, "but it just sounds so much better when you tell it. Promise me, Grannie, promise that you won't ever stop telling me the Pineapple story."

"You know I love you, Gracie, and I always will," said Grannie. "All right, Gracie. Let's go sit together and I will tell you the story of Pineapple again."

CHAPTER ONE

The Dry Field

It had been a very tough and dry year. The grass, if you could find any, was far apart and barely showing its greenness above the ground. As soon as one blade popped out of the ground, it was gone—eaten by some starving animal.

Mama Deer looked at the barren ground all around her. What was she to do? She needed fresh grass so that she could make milk for her little baby. And oh, what a pretty baby she was! She was born on a bright, sunny August day in a large field of corn. The farmer had kept water on the corn during the hot, dry months to help it grow, and this provided a wonderfully cool home for the mother deer and her baby.

But the corn had dried up and wasn't at all tasty to eat. Soon, the farmer would be coming to the field with his monster machines to cut down the corn. Mama Deer knew this. She would have to find a new home for her and the baby.

Mama Deer and Baby Deer ventured out at night when it was safe. Mama Deer taught Baby Deer how to look for food in the brushland around the river while the humans were sound asleep in their funny nests. Some of their nests were built from the wood of the trees in the brushland, and some were built from the rocks on the ground and in the river. Mama Deer could never figure out why these humans had to go to so much trouble to build a nest when they could have easily laid in the coolness and shade of the big oak trees or the corn fields.

Baby Deer and Mama Deer traveled long distances at night, looking for grass to satisfy their hunger. They always finished their nightly feast near the

nest of some humans that lived right at the river's edge, which was far from their corn field home. Their dessert would be the different plants that grew in the ground around the humans' nest. They were the tastiest of all.

The time came for the farmer to cut down the corn, and Baby Deer and Mama Deer lost their home. But Mama Deer remembered how wonderful the plants tasted at the humans' nest on the river. So during the day Baby Deer and Mama Deer hid out in the brushland. Then at nightfall they would sneak into the humans' yard to have their fill of the luscious plants.

Getting to that special place was somewhat difficult for Baby Deer. Mama Deer would gracefully jump over the highest of fences to get to the humans' nest by the river. It was more difficult for Baby Deer, who had to run up and down the fence line looking for the tiniest hole to crawl through. It wasn't long before the little deer found a secret hole. She wanted to be as graceful a jumper as her mama someday, but for now, a hole in the fence would have to do. Sometimes they would race and Baby Deer would make it to the river nest before her mama could. Of course, Mama Deer just pretended to lose.

After they had their nightly fill, they would bed down in the coolness of the grass and the safe darkness of the night. Early in the morning, just before the humans came out of their nest, Baby Deer and her mama would leave for the brushland to hide in it during the heat of the day. They did this every night, at least for a few weeks. Life was good. Mama Deer and her little baby had a new home, and they were very happy. At night, they would dance to the rhythm of their animal world as they watched the twinkling stars and listened to the gentle breezes all around them.

The River

Mama Deer knew she must teach her baby how to survive. There was always the possibility that some day or some night, Mama Deer might not come back to her darling little baby. Always in the shadows of their animal world were the dangers of getting hit by a car or going hungry. The danger of getting a leg caught in wire while jumping over a fence, or catching some animal disease, was always present. Worse yet was the fear and the smell of the hunter that always came with the cold blast of winter wind.

Early one evening, while Baby Deer was still very young, Mama Deer went on a scouting trip to look for a new source of food—but she did not come back. Mama Deer had told Baby Deer to stay hidden in the brush until she came back. So, being a good little deer, Baby Deer did what her mama told her to do. She waited and waited. No Mama Deer! As each day passed by, Baby Deer got weaker and weaker, and she knew she needed food. She missed her mama.

Where is she? Why doesn't she come home? I want her . . . I need her . . . I love her. These thoughts kept creeping through Baby Deer's mind as she lay in hiding, getting weaker and weaker. Soon she could hardly hold herself up when she tried to stand, and her legs could barely move. Sadness crept over her as she realized that her mama was probably never coming home again. A tear rolled down the side of her little cheek as she thought of her lost mama. Her mama had kept her warm at night and always had plenty of good-tasting milk for her to drink. But Baby Deer was by herself now, and she had to figure out what to do if she were to survive.

She thought about that river nest where she spent many glorious nights with her mama. The food was good there. The trees had good shade, and the grass made a nice bed to lie on. The humans that lived there seemed nice enough. *What did they call each other? Oh yes,* she thought, *I think they called each other Grannie and Grandpa.*

The big human was Grandpa. He always left early in the morning so that he could feed the baby calves in the pasture next to the river nest. Grannie loved animals too, and she was always playing with a little frankfurter dog they called Belle and the five pretty horses they called Hollywood, Chapa, Bob, Parkay, and Max. Baby Deer's mind was spinning fast. *Maybe I can go there. Maybe they will help me. Maybe they will even love me like my Mama.*

She slowly got up on her wobbly little legs and took her first step towards the path that led to the river nest. It took her a while to make the next step. She knew she was in danger of dying. Would she make it? She took one step, then another, as her struggling body tried to do what her mind was willing it to do. She heard Belle faintly barking in the distance. She slowly kept going, step by step, getting weaker and weaker. She could see the river nest. She found her secret hole and was barely able to get through it. Baby Deer feebly walked on. Soon she was in the yard. Should she go further? Her hunger and weakness had taken all the fear of humans out of her. She was dying; what could be worse than that?

She came to the porch. She barely made it to the front step before she collapsed, still about six feet from the door. *This is it. It is over,* she thought. She did not have a single ounce of energy left in her tiny, frail body. Nearby, Belle picked up her head from a deep morning nap under an old oak tree and sniffed the air. The smell of death softly drifted through the air. Belle saw the deer and started to bark.

Suddenly the door opened, and a very surprised Grannie looked down and said, "Oh my goodness! What do we have here?"

Chapter Three

The Farm

Grannie bent down and looked at the frail little deer. She got down on her knees and gently patted the baby's head. She placed her ear next to the baby's nose to listen for breathing. Grannie detected a faint breath as she moved her hand down the baby's back. Grannie carefully picked up the little deer, carried her into the house, and placed her on a soft blanket on the living room floor.

Baby Deer could sense what was happening, but she did not have the strength to fight or run away. Grannie covered the baby with a portion of the blanket and went into the kitchen to make a special milk mix for baby animals. She found one of Gracie's old baby bottles and placed the milk mix inside. Next, she warmed the milk so that it might be tastier to eat. Then Grannie lifted Baby Deer's head and placed the nipple into her mouth. No luck: the little deer would not—or could not—suck on the nipple. So Grannie left to look for a very large eyedropper. She found an old one in the kitchen and filled it with the sweet mix of milk. She went back into the living room and began feeding Baby Deer with the large eyedropper. This kind of slow feeding lasted for a couple of days, until the little deer finally began to show signs of recovery.

In the meantime, Grandpa had come home. Grannie told him about Baby Deer, so he proceeded to build a pen under the large oak tree in the front yard. On the third day, Baby Deer slowly got up on her wobbly legs and took a couple of steps. Grannie decided to try the bottle again. This time it worked quite well. That baby was really hungry! Baby Deer was learning to like the taste of that sweet milk mix. For the next three days, Grannie fed the little deer as much as she wanted to eat. After every meal she would take the deer outside for some exercise.

As Baby Deer grew stronger, Grannie and Grandpa started leaving her for a while in the pen. During the heat of the day, they would bring her inside to play. Baby Deer loved to play. She especially enjoyed chasing Belle around the bedroom. Most often, she and Belle would jump up onto the top of the bed or the easy chair and play king of the mountain. It was always a race to see who got there first. Of course, Grannie was not very fond of this game because they played on top of her nice new bedspreads.

One afternoon, Grannie and Grandpa had to check on the new baby calves, so they saddled two horses for the ride to pasture. Max and Parkay were picked for the ride that day. Grannie and Grandpa needed to walk the baby calves to the pens, where they could be marked and given their shots to keep them from getting sick. They would later be separated and sent to different pastures. As Grannie and Grandpa were heading down a narrow trail, they heard noises behind them. Turning to see where the noises were coming from, they saw Belle and her new sidekick, Baby Deer. Those two had decided to follow Grannie and Grandpa to the pasture. Belle and Baby Deer checked out every bush and chased every rabbit they could find. Sometimes they ran ahead of the horses and in and out of the brush. Other times they trotted behind the horses, jumping around and acting silly. They even tried to get the baby calves to run and play with them. That was a fun day and a good day to be an animal on Gilleland Farms.

CHAPTER FOUR

A Little Accident

Looking out the window one hot afternoon, Grannie saw something really funny. She had turned on the sprinklers outside to water the grass since the land was still in the grips of a deep drought. Apparently Baby Deer had invited two of her brushland cousins to come over. They would run and play in the sprinkler, jumping up and chasing each other through the water in circles. It wasn't long before Belle joined in the fun. It was quite a sight to see the three little deer and Belle happily playing in the cool water on a very hot day.

The next morning Grannie walked outside to feed Baby Deer and discovered, to her sadness, that Baby Deer was gone. Grannie searched for the little deer everywhere, in the yard and behind every bush. She called out her name over and over. No Baby Deer. Grannie asked Grandpa to come help in the search. Grandpa drove through the pasture looking for the little deer. No Baby Deer. Even Belle went looking for Baby Deer. Where could she have gone? Grannie and Belle walked down to the river and looked among the rocks and brush. Grannie called out her name. Belle barked and barked. No Baby Deer. Everyone was sad. Even Belle could tell that something was very wrong.

On the third day of Baby Deer's disappearance, Grannie heard Belle furiously barking outside. Wanting to know what the problem was, she

walked toward the back door and looked outside. "Oh my gosh," Grannie shouted with glee.

There stood Baby Deer. She looked very thin from lack of eating, and she had a huge gash on her head. "Where have you been?" Grannie asked.

Of course, the little deer couldn't tell her. It really wasn't Baby Deer's fault. She had just wanted to go out one more time to look for Mama Deer. She still missed her mama very much, especially the warm feeling she would get when she cuddled with her mama at night under the bright, shining stars. By instinct, Baby Deer knew she must go back to her new home when she couldn't find her mama. There she would feel loved and be kept safe. In another time and at another place, she would look again for Mama Deer. But for now, she was happy with her new family.

Baby Deer liked her new home. Her bed was comfortable and the milk was good. The humans seemed nice and loved to play. Belle was quite the companion and a good friend. Together they took many adventurous exploring trips around the house and down to the river. After all, there were many new things to discover.

Later that night, after a very tiring and fun-filled day, Grannie carried the deer outside to her pen. Grannie placed Baby Deer inside her pen and gave her a big kiss on her nose. She rubbed Baby Deer's back and went back inside her nest to take care of Belle and Grandpa. The little deer walked around her pen, and then she settled down for the night on a very comfortable and cool patch of grass. Life was good again. She could tell Grannie and Grandpa loved her. Just before Baby Deer went to sleep, she looked up into the dark night sky. Tonight the stars were twinkling clearly and beautifully. She remembered looking at the stars with her mama what seemed like a long time ago. Then she saw it.

Yes . . . There it was, just as plain as could be. Scattered in the dark night sky above, twinkling stars spelled out the words, "I love you, Baby Deer." Baby Deer knew these beautiful stars were her Mama's way of talking to her. Feeling the love of her mother all around her, Baby Deer smiled and slowly drifted off into a peaceful sleep.

Chapter Five

Grace

The next day, Grannie and Grandpa were buzzing all over the place. They were excited because their granddaughter, Grace, whom they called Gracie, was coming to visit. Gracie lived near the city with her mom and dad. Gracie's dad was Grannie and Grandpa's son, and they loved him very much. Gracie loved her parents very much, and she also loved her Grannie and Grandpa. But mostly, at age three, Gracie loved animals.

Finally Gracie arrived with a lot of hoopla and fanfare and hugging and kissing. Gracie said, "I told you I was coming on Monday." Of course, it was really Saturday, but then again, time is always lost on a three-year-old.

Off in the pen in the corner of the yard, the little deer silently watched and observed all the events that were unfolding. *This little human must be very important to these people,* thought the little deer. *Maybe she will like me too and be my new number one best friend.* Belle had been Baby Deer's number one best friend. Now with Gracie arriving, Belle might have to move over and become Baby Deer's number two best friend.

Gracie ran around giving everyone their special hugs and kisses and then bent down to lay a big smooch on Belle. Belle loved all the attention that Gracie always gave her when she came to visit. Gracie's visits also meant

that Belle would have to take a good long bath—that is, if she wanted to crawl into bed with Gracie and sleep at her feet. There they would snuggle together, along with all six baby dolls, and drift off into a long night's sleep.

All the while, Baby Deer was watching. Gracie noticed the new pen in the front yard, and then she noticed the little animal. She went running and screaming with glee towards the pen with Belle tagging along behind her. Gracie shouted, "I can't believe my eyes."

All the commotion scared Baby Deer, who ran into the fence and got a little cut on her face. Grannie calmly walked over to the pen and picked up the deer to calm her down. Then Gracie started petting her. She touched the hurt spot on Baby Deer's face and said she was sorry and that the hurt would get better. Then Gracie bent down and kissed the little deer's cut, and the friendship began.

This time, Belle was doing the watching. Gracie turned to Grannie and Grandpa and asked what the deer's name was. Grannie said she didn't have one and told Gracie that when her daddy was little, he had called his baby deer Peaches. So, thinking that all baby deer had to be named after fruit—because that is how three-year-olds think—Gracie named the new baby deer Pineapple. And that is how Baby Deer got her name.

Gracie spent that weekend playing with Belle and feeding her new friend Pineapple. The three of them had so much fun together. They played chase around the house. Then they would run through the house, jumping up on top of the bed or chair and playing king of the mountain. It was hard to tell who was more excited: Grace, Pineapple, or Belle. After a hard day at play, they all came inside and lay down on the living room floor. They huddled tightly together, laying all over each other, watching "It's Tickle Torture Time" on television. It was hard to separate them. The three of them had become glue.

CHAPTER SIX

Best Friends

This friendship continued for several more visits out to the farm. They had so much fun playing together that even the horses, Hollywood, Bob, Chapa, Parkay, and Max, would get excited as they stood at the fence watching Gracie and her animal friends playing outside. The "five kings," as Grannie called the horses, were doing their best trying to figure out why this little human was so special. She would always bring such excitement to the farm. Why, she could get Grannie and Grandpa to do almost anything. The "kings" would patiently wait by their feed troughs to see who would be the "chosen one" that day to carry the precious little princess around on his back. They always tried to be on their best behavior when Gracie showed up, and whoever was chosen would be very careful with such special cargo. They each would continuously look back to see if Gracie was still riding high and straight in the saddle.

One day when Belle and Pineapple were playing outside, they both got a little too close to the swimming pool. They were chasing each other, and before you knew it, they both fell in. What a sight! Such splashing and carrying on you've never seen. Grannie saw the whole episode unfold, and she calmly bent down and retrieved both wet balls of hair out of the pool.

They looked so funny . . . kind of like wet rats. For the next few days, Belle and Pineapple were very cautious around the edge of the pool. But since the weather was still very hot, it wasn't long before the two animal friends decided they needed to get back into the pool. They did, and this time they weren't scared. They even figured out how to use the steps to get in and out.

Pineapple was growing, and Gracie really wanted her to come to town and live at her house. The grown-ups talked about it and decided that bringing Pineapple to Gracie's house would be a good thing. So late one evening Grannie and Grandpa loaded Pineapple into the back seat of the pickup. Belle was watching and wanted to go too. It was decided, however, that it wouldn't be a very good idea. Belle would miss Pineapple, but they would get to visit each other again later.

Grandpa started the pickup, Grannie got into the backseat with Pineapple, and off they went to town. Grannie tried to keep Pineapple down in the seat, but she was much too curious for that. Pineapple kept popping up and down, trying to look out the windows. As they left the farm, Pineapple began to see that something very different was happening. She put her little nose up against the back window and looked out at her friends and all that had been hers to enjoy. As they drove further away from the farm, Pineapple had no idea that her life was going to change; she would no longer be a country deer. It didn't even occur to Pineapple that she was going to stay with Gracie and become a modern city deer.

CHAPTER SEVEN

The City Deer

The trip to town was filled with many new things to see. Pineapple wondered where she was going, but she felt comfortable that Grannie and Grandpa would protect her. When they arrived closer to town, she saw more humans and nests than she had ever seen before. *Where is the brushland?* she thought.

They drove a little further out and came to a place where the nests were further apart and separated by large patches of brush. Soon the pickup stopped in front of a pretty nest, and Grandpa got out and opened the door for Grannie and Pineapple.

Pineapple looked at the door of the nest, and it suddenly flew open. Out ran her number one best friend, Gracie, waving her arms and shouting with glee. As Gracie hugged and kissed Pineapple, the little deer thought that this city thing might not be so bad after all. Gracie's mom was busy in the kitchen learning how to make the sweet mix of milk. Her dad had just finished building a new pen for Pineapple to live in. Later, when Pineapple knew to stay close by, they would let her roam freely.

Gracie was excited and wanted to run and play with her friend Pineapple. After a good visit and some very sad good-byes, Grannie and Grandpa slowly got back into the pickup to go home. They hoped that Pineapple would always remember them. They loved the little deer and would greatly

miss her. But now Gracie and her mom and dad would love and care for Pineapple. As Grannie and Grandpa drove back to the farm, they couldn't stop thinking about how very hard it was to let go.

Now that Pineapple was a city deer, she had a lot of new things to learn. Gracie's dad carried Pineapple over to her new pen and carefully placed her inside. Pineapple still wasn't sure what was happening. She only knew that she was not with Grannie and Grandpa at her country home. Gracie's mom carefully and lovingly tried to feed Pineapple with a new bottle of milk, but Pineapple wanted her old bottle and her Grannie to feed her. Gracie's mom and dad wondered what they could do to get Pineapple to eat. Even having Gracie in the pen with Pineapple did not help. Gracie's dad knew they needed help, so he called Grannie and Grandpa just as they were arriving back at their farm.

Wanting to help out, Grandpa told Grannie to find an old T-shirt and spray it with her perfume and rub it on her arms. This was an old trick that Grandpa had used many times with orphaned animals on the farm. With the shirt in hand, they got back in the pickup and drove to town. Once there, Grannie and Grandpa quickly walked to the pen and began to pet Pineapple. Grannie picked up Pineapple and gave her a big hug. Pineapple was so glad to see her Grannie and Grandpa again. She quickly began giving Grannie many wet kisses all over her neck and face. Gracie's mom and dad saw this and immediately felt better. Grandpa took the shirt, wrapped it around the bottle, and tried to feed Pineapple again. This time it worked, and Pineapple began eating again. The comfortable feelings and the familiar smells of back home made Pineapple feel good. It made her want to fill her hungry belly again.

Now everybody was happy, and Gracie decided that her Grannie and Grandpa could do anything. Of course, Gracie already knew her Grannie thought that if Grandpa wanted to, he could rope the moon. Now Gracie had proof. With this problem taken care of, it wasn't long before Pineapple was feeling very good about her new life in the city.

CHAPTER EIGHT

The Neighborhood

Pineapple spent many happy days frolicking in the grass with Gracie and all of her pet friends. There was Twinkie, the short-legged mutt who seemed to have the number one position in the house. There was Jet, the sleek black cat who was always watching Gracie and lurking around every corner. Scarlet was the grumpy old gray-haired cat who really didn't like to do much of anything. And of course, there was Midge, the big black Lab, who had, by the way, gotten very, very fat. Last but not least was Lola the Rat. She wasn't really a rat, just a tiny, hairy Chihuahua who liked standing underneath the big dogs and sitting up high on top of the couch.

It was always such a sight in the small neighborhood outside of town to see Sylvia, Gracie's nanny, take her for a ride down the road. Sylvia loved Gracie. She would put Gracie in her wagon and off they would go down the middle of the road. Following them in a row and always in the same order were Twinkie, Jet, Midge, Lola, Scarlet, and bringing up the end of the line, Pineapple. The neighbors would get quite a chuckle at this little parade that took place almost every day.

Soon, a close friendship formed between Midge and Pineapple. Midge had been a rescue dog and had not known many happy days before she

came to live with Gracie's parents. Jet had just shown up at the house one afternoon and decided that he would stay. Twinkie had been the neighborhood dog at Gracie's mom and dad's old house. After eating at all the different houses and spending many nights in different beds, Twinkie decided that she had the best deal with Gracie's mom and dad. So Twinkie promptly moved in with them. Grannie found the starving Scarlet on the farm. Grannie gave her plenty to eat, and then she called Gracie's dad to come and take the old cat to the shelter. Scarlet never made the trip; she ended up living with Gracie and her parents, who thought they could get rid of Scarlet's grumpiness. They were wrong. Nobody knows where Lola the Rat came from . . . and that's a fact.

Pineapple loved Gracie's sandbox. Many afternoons Pineapple could be found bedded down in the coolness of the sand. Gracie would be there putting sand in her bucket and pouring it all over Pineapple. Of course, Pineapple didn't mind a bit because Gracie was her number one best friend. Everywhere Gracie would go, Pineapple would follow, and whatever Gracie wanted to do was just fine with Pineapple.

The only problem that Gracie's mom and dad had with Pineapple was that she would go onto the porch and eat all of their beautiful plants. Then Pineapple would visit the neighbors and eat all of their beautiful plants for dessert. It wasn't really Pineapple's fault. Those tasty plants simply couldn't be resisted. The neighbors weren't always happy with Pineapple, but they knew she brought many happy smiles and shouts of glee from the children of the neighborhood, especially Aubrey and Ashtyn. They lived in the house next door to Gracie, and they always had a great time playing together with Pineapple.

Chapter Nine

Something New

One day Grandpa was eating lunch at Yomi's Café in Batesville and talking with Lester, a neighbor of Gracie's mom and dad. Yomi's was a good place for all the farmers and ranchers in the area to eat lunch and talk about all that was happening. Grandpa always said that the man who chose the third stool at the counter was never wrong with his information.

Lester was telling Grandpa how Pineapple and Midge would always come over in the late afternoon and walk with him down the road. Lester had been very sick and had to go to the hospital. The doctor told him that he needed to walk every day to gain back his strength. He told Grandpa he always enjoyed the company of Midge and Pineapple on his walks, and he had many good laughs watching their antics.

Then Lester told Grandpa what had happened earlier that morning while it was still dark. Lester and his wife woke up to a loud noise outside in their backyard. They peeked out of a window and saw, to their surprise, Pineapple. She had gotten into their pool and was swimming around. Pineapple made two leisurely laps around the pool and then swam over to the steps, climbed out, and shook off the water like a dog. She proceeded to walk over to the

flower bed by the pool and munch on the delicious flowers. After she had her fill, she walked over to a collapsed lounge chair and lay down on top of it. She had always loved playing in the pool with Belle at her country home, and Lester could tell that this wasn't her first trip to his swimming pool, nor would it be her last. After a few minutes, she slowly got up and trotted back to her house. There she would anxiously wait for the sun to come up and for little Gracie to come bounding out the back door to play. *Ah,* Pineapple thought, *life just doesn't get any better than this.*

Time went on. Pineapple kept getting bigger, and Gracie was soon four and then almost five. A very special bond tightly formed between this beautiful little girl and her once-wild little country deer. Gracie was now in pre-K. Big Stuff! Every day she would go to school, and her animal friends would wait patiently for her to come home for lunch. You could always find them waiting around the front porch for their special friend to come home and play. Gracie was learning a lot of new and wonderful things in school, including a new foreign language. Pineapple was having a really hard time trying to understand this new language. *Just what does "nana nana boo boo" mean, anyway?* thought Pineapple. *And what about "liar, liar, pants on fire?" Whose pants?*

One day Gracie came home from school very sick. She did not get to go outside and play for a whole week. Everyone was worried about her. Even Pineapple and her other animal friends knew something was wrong. They continued to wait outside the door for Gracie to come out and play. Finally Gracie started feeling better, and she got to spend the weekend with her Grannie and Grandpa.

Belle was excited because her special friend had come back to play. Then Grandpa got sick. Gracie told Grannie that it looked like her bad tummy had traveled all the way down her leg, out her shoe, and into Grandpa. Grandpa laughed and soon started feeling better too. After a fun-filled weekend, Gracie went back home.

Gracie needed a new pair of shoes. She was getting ready for her first violin recital and she wanted to look her best. She had been taking lessons

and learning to play for two years. But there were still a lot of weird sounds and squeaks coming out of her violin. Sometimes her mom and dad would suggest that she go outside for a while and play her violin for Pineapple. Gracie loved doing this because Pineapple didn't care about the squeaks and always liked what she played, especially "Mississippi Hot Dog."

One day Gracie, Pineapple, Twinkie, and Lola were sitting down watching TV. Gracie had scattered her toys everywhere. Gracie's dad walked in and told her it was time to pick up all of her toys. Gracie made a wise comment back to her dad. He walked over to Gracie and said, "What did you say to me?"

Pineapple had not yet seen Gracie's dad act this way; she could tell that Gracie was in big trouble. Then Gracie told her dad, "I was talking China, Dad. I don't even know what I said, but I will pick up those toys right now."

Chuckling and shaking his head in amazement, Gracie's dad sat back down in his chair. Pineapple looked over at Gracie and thought, *Phew, that was close.*

Change

Gracie and Pineapple shared many special times together in the country and in the city. Gracie loved her Pineapple, and Pineapple loved and watched over Gracie. Every once in a while, however, a thought would come to Pineapple. A stirring in her heart told her that she still longed to see her mama and her fun-loving cousins. Pineapple was growing up, and sooner or later she might have to go look just one more time for her animal family. As the fun days of summer slowly passed, Pineapple knew she would soon have to make a very important decision.

That day finally arrived. Gracie was playing in her sandbox and Pineapple was grazing on some tender new grass. Pineapple sensed something and looked up. She saw movement in the brush. She peered out in the distance and thought she saw another deer in the shadows of the black brush. Pineapple wanted to go see who was out there, but she was desperately torn by her love for little Gracie and the love of her own kind. Pineapple looked at Gracie, still happily playing in her sandbox. The call of the wild was getting stronger and harder to resist. Although it broke her heart, Pineapple decided to leave. She walked slowly to the edge of the yard, looked back at Gracie with loving, caring eyes, and then slowly drifted out of sight into the shadows of the thick, black brush . . . and Gracie didn't even know.

Epilogue

Mama Deer and Gracie would forever be the shadows of Pineapple's heart. Having Pineapple for a friend and playmate taught Gracie a lot about life. They showed each other how animals and people can both have an unconditional love for each other, no matter what.

In a few short months, Gracie learned the importance of love, kindness, and letting go. There will be a time in your life that you will have to say good-bye to something or someone you love. You do this so that they can live the life they were meant to live. It is a sad but beautiful thing to love something so much that you can give it its freedom.

This faith in love, kindness, and friendship between humans and animals is what life is really all about. Instead of thinking about your problems in life, think of how you can make life nicer for someone else. As we all get older, we come to a point in our lives when we realize what really matters. The lessons we learn in life will in time show all of us what we have always known deep in our hearts to be right.

Gracie, sometimes the lessons you learn will hurt and cause you to fail. Just wipe away those tears and put your hurt behind you; get back up and try again and again, and know that your Grannie and Grandpa will always love you, no matter what.

We are all given special moments in time that allow us an opportunity to show our love and kindness to the people and animals around us. Maybe if we take advantage of these special moments, this spirit of life that we all share will shine through and make all of us the best we could ever be.

Gracie . . . Who are the shadows of your heart?

About the Author

BackRoadImages.net

Linda Gilleland, a retired school teacher, grew up in an agricultural family and graduated from college with a dual degree in sociology and elementary education. She has always loved the outdoors and animals—horses in particular. The first and most-loved book that she ever owned was *Bambi*, and as a young girl she was always bringing home stray animals. She married her husband, Bruce, and moved to the family farm and ranch in 1970. She has a wonderful son, Rader, an equally wonderful daughter-in-law, Hollie, and two beautiful grandchildren, Grace and Jack. She has been involved in many community service, school, and 4-H projects throughout her lifetime.

Originally, Linda wanted to write this story as a gift for her granddaughter, Grace. She wanted Grace to remember her legacy of agricultural life and how life used to be on the farm as Grace grew older and started her own family. Through this story, Linda wanted Grace to remember what life is really all about. This faith in love, kindness, and friendship between people and animals can be carried over into our individual lives and will give all of us, in time, many opportunities to make life nicer for someone else. So, with the encouragement of her husband and friends, Linda became an unintended author.

About the Artist

Leigh Ann Irish grew up in south Texas and moved to Shreveport, Louisiana, in 2011 following her marriage to Lyn Irish. She has been drawing and painting since childhood. Formal training included commercial art and illustration classes at Austin Community College. After a few years of working as a graphic artist/illustrator she became a full-time mother and homemaker, only drawing or painting occasionally until 2003, when her children were grown and she had time to pursue her art again.

Since then she has devoted most of her time and talent to commissioned portraits but continues to do occasional illustrations and other drawings and paintings. Recent awards include Best of Show at the regional art competition, show, and sale sponsored by the Uvalde Visual Arts League in 2009 and 2010 Artist of the Year at the Coppini Academy of Fine Arts in San Antonio, Texas. Her work is displayed in several small galleries in south Texas. Her work can also be seen on her website (with her previous name) at www.LeighAnnSanderlinArt.com.

Urth Studio